Before Margaret
Met The Pope

The Pope's **CAT** series!

*The story of a stray that was born
on the Via della Conciliazione in Rome,
adopted by the Pope, and how she then runs
the Vatican from museum to floorboard.
For ages six and up.*

This volume was preceded by

The Pope's Cat

Margaret's Night in St. Peter's (A Christmas Story)

Margaret's First Holy Week

Margaret and the Pope Go to Assisi

Before Margaret Met The Pope

A Conclave Story

JON M. SWEENEY
Illustrated by ROY DELEON

PARACLETE PRESS
BREWSTER, MASSACHUSETTS

△ △

2021 First Printing
Before Margaret Met the Pope:
A Conclave Story

Text copyright © 2021 by Jon M. Sweeney
Illustrations copyright © 2021
by Roy DeLeon

ISBN 978-1-64060-502-2

This is a work of fiction. The author
has used the real titles of Pope and Holy
Father in the sense in which they are normally
understood: for the leader of the Roman Catholic
Church who resides in Vatican City; but no historical
Pope or Holy Father, past or present, is intended.

The Paraclete Press name and logo (dove on cross) are trade-
marks of Paraclete Press, Inc.

Names: Sweeney, Jon M., 1967- author. | DeLeon, Roy, illustrator.
Title: Before Margaret met the Pope : a conclave story / Jon M. Sweeney ;
illustrated by Roy DeLeon. | Description: Brewster, Massachusetts :
Paraclete Press, 2021. | Series: The Pope's cat ; 5
Audience: Ages 7-12. | Audience: Grades 2-3. | Summary:
A stray cat sneaks into the Sistine Chapel and watches as her friend is
elected Supreme Pontiff.
Identifiers: LCCN 2020044730 (print) | LCCN 2020044731 (ebook) | ISBN
9781640605022 | ISBN 9781640605039 (epub) | ISBN 9781640605046 (pdf)
Subjects: CYAC: Cats--Fiction. | Popes--Fiction. | Catholics--Fiction. |
Christian life--Fiction. | Vatican City--Fiction.
Classification: LCC PZ7.1.S9269 Be 2021 (print) | LCC PZ7.1.S9269 (ebook)
| DDC [E]--dc23
LC record available at https://lccn.loc.gov/2020044730
LC ebook record available at https://lccn.loc.gov/2020044731.

10 9 8 7 6 5 4 3 2 1

Published by Paraclete Press, Brewster, Massachusetts
www.paracletepress.com

Manufactured by PRINPIA Co., Ltd. 54,
Gasanro 9-Gil, Geumcheon-gu,
Seoul 08513, Korea
Printed in September 2021, Seoul, South Korea

For Pope Francis,

Viva il Papa

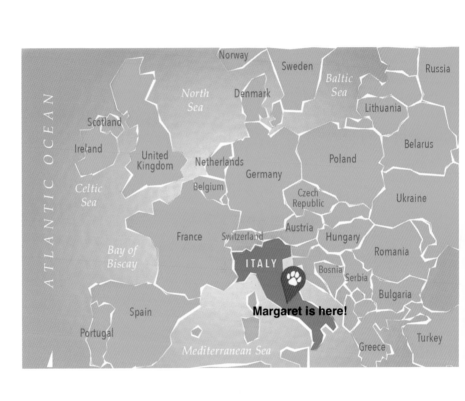

Margaret is here!

CHAPTER 1

Before Margaret met the Pope, she lived on the streets of Rome. She was a small cat in one of the busiest, most crowded cities in all Europe.

Rome is the capital of Italy. More than 4 million people live there.

Rome surrounds Vatican City, the world's tiniest country, and home to the Pope, the Curia, and the Swiss Guard.

Margaret had lots of friends on the Via della Conciliazione. There were the restaurant owners who set out plates of leftovers by the back doors of their restaurants. Margaret loved their dishes of fish and clams, lasagna and alfredo, or just about anything they had to give her that day.

There were other cats in the neighborhood, too, with whom Margaret often played. They usually got along well.

There were even dogs that were friendly to her, and then there were some that were not so friendly.

One time, Margaret was chased by a really big dog that she was convinced wanted to eat her.

He would have caught her, too, had she not crossed under a wooden fence and slipped under the feet of people in line, waiting to enter the Vatican Museums.

She had many adventures, not all of them scary, like that one. Most of the time, her life in Rome was exciting.

The Via della Conciliazione connects Rome to the tiny world that is found inside Vatican City; it is a short street that links St. Peter's Square to the banks of the Tiber River, and beyond.

Along the Conciliazione are shops selling postcards and rosary beads and figurines of Popes and Saints, and gelato shops where children leave with delicious cones of gelato that drip onto the sidewalk on hot summer afternoons. There was Margaret, following those kids, licking up those drips!

Cats like people. They don't usually come when you call them by name, as dogs do, but cats like to be noticed, to be patted on the head, or scratched gently under the chin.

Margaret would often meet children on the streets of Rome.

On Wednesdays, she would sometimes walk down the Conciliazione to St. Peter's Square, where children and their families would gather, with others, to see the Pope at his regular weekly address.

The Square would be full of people from all over the world. Everyone wanted to see the Pope. On summer days, many people would wear hats because it's hot in Rome in June, July, and August. But despite the heat, they would sit or stand for hours, happy to see and cheer, and listen to what the Pope had to say.

Back then, Margaret didn't know the Pope. She only knew that he was the person everyone seemed to be talking about.

Then, one day, the Pope died.

CHAPTER 2

Newspapers all over the world, in every country, ran big headlines:

The Pope is dead.

Television crews covered St. Peter's Square and the Via della Conciliazione with their trucks, cameras, and equipment. Reporters with microphones were everywhere, interviewing priests in white collars, friars in white, black, or brown habits or robes, cardinals with red caps, and religious sisters, asking each to reflect on the life and papacy of the Holy Father who had died, and to speculate on what might happen next.

"The apostolic successor of St. Peter has died," Margaret overheard one sister say.

"What does 'apostolic successor' mean?" asked a reporter.

"There has been a direct line of Popes since Jesus Christ made St. Peter, one of the original apostles, the first Pope, almost 2,000 years ago. The next Pope will be the next in that apostolic succession," the sister said.

"So, what happens next?" another reporter asked.

"Within a week, our Holy Father will be buried, and we will honor him. A week after that, and there will be a conclave to elect the next Pope," Margaret heard the sister say.

Now, keep in mind: the Pope who died was not the Pope who adopted Margaret off the streets of Rome. The Pope who died was the Pope *before* Margaret's Pope was elected in a conclave.

There's that word again.

Conclave.

It sounds strange, Margaret thought to herself.

Conclave comes from two Latin words. Everything Catholic used to come from Latin words! Put them together and those two Latin words mean "with key."

cum "with"
+ *clavis* "key"
_____

"with key"

What are keys used for? To lock things.

In other words, a conclave is a kind of secret.

Popes are elected in conclaves by the College of Cardinals, and College of Cardinals is the name given to all the Cardinals of the Roman Catholic Church. They gather in one big, locked room until they are done electing the next Pope.

Soon, Margaret would know how conclaves work—because she would be there to see one happen.

Most people don't know this about Margaret. Before the Pope adopted her, even before he met her one morning while out for a walk on the Via della Conciliazione, Margaret watched as he was elected the successor of St. Peter.

CHAPTER 3

Many of the Roman or Papal Curia—the people who assist the Pope in administrating all the congregations, councils, and offices of the universal Roman Catholic Church—were anxious and upset in the days leading up to the conclave.

The Pope had died, which was upsetting. Plus, there was a lot to be done in the days ahead. After the sorrow of a Pope dying, there is the work and the excitement of a conclave.

Margaret began to observe all this activity when, once again, she slipped under that wooden fence barricade where people were lining up to enter the Vatican Museums.

Only one person, a young girl, seemed to pay any attention when a stray cat snuck past the Swiss Guards approaching the Museum entrance.

"Mom!" she said. But by the time her mom stopped talking, and turned her head to look, there was nothing to see.

Soon, Margaret was inside. She was curious.

Vatican City is like a fortress. Centuries ago, soldiers fought to try and get inside, and usually they failed.

How did Margaret get in? She slipped under that barricade and ran fast-as-a-cat past one last Swiss Guard man who was staring straight ahead. Guards are not trained to notice cats.

She wasn't interested in the Museums. Cats don't usually notice paintings and sculptures and tapestries. So Margaret kept walking from gallery to gallery.

By the time she entered the fifth gallery, she began to wonder how many there were all together. (She didn't know yet that there are fifty-four!)

She noticed a janitor's cart and an empty pail at the bottom of it. She jumped in the pail and was happy to discover that it wasn't full of water.

Pulling a towel over her head, Margaret hoped that no one would see her inside.

The janitor had finished her work for the day. So she pushed her cart, without knowing Margaret was inside it, through the rest of the galleries.

Then she stopped at the very last one, to talk with someone.

Margaret was afraid to peek out from behind the towel. She didn't want anyone to see her, and she didn't want to get in trouble.

She also didn't want to leave. If someone found her inside the Vatican, they would surely take her back outside.

So she sat, and she sat. It felt like hours that she sat in that dark space, until finally, she got up the courage to look out.

First, Margaret saw another Swiss Guard. Then she saw another. She didn't know any of them, then.

The Swiss Guards were standing at attention, with spears in their hands, in front of two very large wooden doors. They looked fearsome! Margaret thought their colorful uniforms were pretty.

The doors were as big and tall as elephants.

A sign read, "The Sistine Chapel."

Little did Margaret know, then, that the Sistine Chapel is the place where conclaves take place.

One of the most famous churches in the world—with a ceiling painted by Michelangelo—the Sistine Chapel is usually on the tour, but it wasn't on this day.

This day, the Chapel was being prepared for the conclave that was about to begin.

There were many people walking quietly in and out, carrying boards of wood and chairs. Margaret even saw stoves. What would they be used for, in a conclave, she wondered? *Perhaps to cook pizza!* she thought. (But that doesn't sound right.)

Dozens of people were preparing the famous room for the conclave that was about to take place.

And soon those elephant-sized doors would be closed and locked—"with key"—with only the Cardinals inside.

CHAPTER 4

While all those people were making all those preparations for the Cardinals to enter the Sistine Chapel and begin the conclave, Margaret began to ponder what she should do next.

The janitor's cart wasn't going to be sitting there for long.

She saw that workers were constructing a wooden floor over the top of the marble floor that tourists and pilgrims see on the tour. "We need to protect the Chapel," Margaret heard someone say.

Then, long tables and chairs, enough to sit 120 members of the College of Cardinals, were carried inside.

And in the center of the room, workers began to install not just one, but two, of those stoves she had seen earlier. *Pizza!* Margaret again pondered excitedly. She really needed lunch by now.

"There was at least one occasion when a stove scratched this beautiful floor!" a supervising member of the Curia remarked. "That won't happen again."

Just then, Margaret saw the perfect place to hide: under a portion of that new wooden floor. She looked around and, when she saw that no one was watching, she ran. Reaching that secret spot at the other end of the room in a couple of seconds, she then tucked herself neatly inside.

Once she was there, and knew that no one had seen her, she promptly fell asleep. ZZzz.

Margaret was way overdue for a cat nap. She had had a very busy day.

When she woke up hours later, it was to the sound of chanting. She had never heard chanting before. She didn't really even know, at that time, what prayer was.

What she was hearing was the College of Cardinals chanting and praying what is called the Litany of the Saints, as they processed their way toward the now-ready Sistine Chapel.

Perhaps you have heard the Litany of the Saints before. It may not be new to you, as it was to a stray cat from Rome.

It is a prayer that Catholics pray to appeal to the holy fathers, mothers, brothers, and sisters who have lived before us, and who now are in heaven praying for us. It can be a long prayer, and when chanted, it is very beautiful.

The Cardinals were singing the Litany of the Saints as they walked toward where Margaret was hiding:

Holy Mary, pray for us...
All the holy Angels, pray for us...
Saint Joseph, pray for us...
Saints Francis and Dominic, pray for us...
Saint Teresa, pray for us...

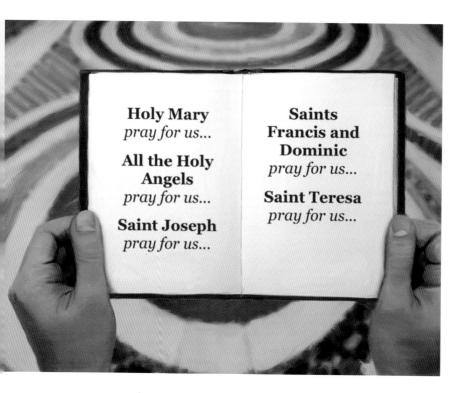

Margaret peeked her head out from her corner to see what was happening.

She saw Cardinals entering the Chapel.

They finished their prayer, and began to find their places at the tables, each one behind a small placard with his name on it.

But they didn't sit down.

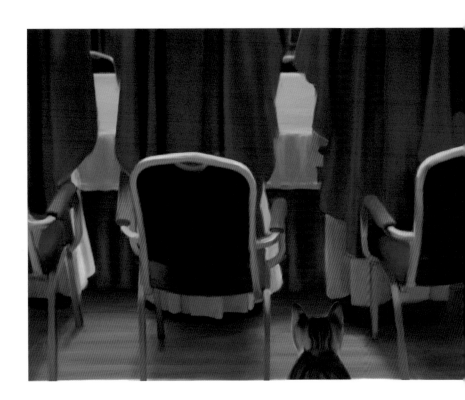

First, each removed his red hat and placed it on the table in front of him. It was then that Margaret saw how each Cardinal was wearing another red hat! The hat they removed is called a *biretta* – it has square corners and is more ceremonial.

The hat left on each cardinal's head is a cap, a *zucchetto*, like the Pope wears, although his is always white. A cardinal's *zucchetto* is red. It looks like a pumpkin cut in half and dyed red.

Why is it red? Because a cardinal is supposed to remember that he gives everything he has, even his blood, if necessary, to the service of the Church.

Then they began lining up behind a podium and taking turns to say an oath of faithfulness to the Church, and to the conclave. Each Cardinal promised to faithfully serve as Pope if he was the one elected.

What happened next scared Margaret.

"*Extra omnes*," someone loudly said, and Margaret jumped. She was startled.

She didn't know that that Latin phrase means "Everyone out," but she could sense the meaning because everyone who wasn't dressed like a Cardinal—monks, sisters, priests, friars, bishops, men and women in suits—even four people with cameras and microphones, because the Cardinals' oaths were apparently shown on television—began to quickly leave.

Was she supposed to go too? She shook her head to herself. *I'm staying put*, she purred.

Then those elephant-sized doors closed with a loud rattling sound. There were several Swiss Guards standing outside, at strict attention, and they didn't move a bit even when those doors were slammed shut.

Only Cardinals, and Margaret, were left inside.

What did she see?

All 120 Cardinals sat down and listened to a homily. The Cardinal giving the homily urged them to listen for the guidance of the Holy Spirit. Everyone was quiet.

Just then, something tickled Margaret's nose and she felt like she was going to sneeze. She held her breath. But still the sneeze was coming! So she put her paw to her nose and closed her eyes tightly. A few seconds went by. No sneeze. The feeling slowly went away. *Whew!* she thought, *that was close!*

A little while later, the Cardinals voted for the first time.

Seated at those long tables, Margaret saw as each one used a pen to write on a ballot. Each ballot had Latin writing at the top:

"*Eligo in Summum Pontificem…*" ("I elect as Supreme Pontiff…")

When all the Cardinals had written the name of a person they thought most capable of being Pope, they folded their paper twice. (That way no one could see what was written inside.) Each walked up to the Chapel altar and placed his card in a goblet.

The votes were then counted by three Cardinals. They tallied the votes one by one.

Three other Cardinals took a needle and string and poked a hole in each ballot, to show that it had been counted, and then strung the ballots together. *How pretty*, thought Margaret. Then they placed the used ballots in one of the stoves in the middle of the room.

Margaret smiled, although none of the Cardinals could see her smiling. She wanted to play with the string.

They burned the ballots in the stove! *No pizza*, Margaret sighed.

One person must win the votes of two-thirds of the College of Cardinals, to be elected Pope. That first vote named nine different people, and the most votes anyone received was thirty.

With 120 Cardinal-electors voting, one person had to receive eighty votes.

It would take four more ballots before that happened—before the Cardinals came to an agreement by voting a two-thirds majority for one person. Of course, it was Margaret's Pope who was elected that day.

Every time the Cardinals burned unsuccessful ballots in the stove, Margaret found that, again, she felt like she was going to sneeze. She kept holding her breath and covering her face with her paws! It turns out that Margaret is allergic to smoke.

When the Pope was elected, the Cardinals burned the ballots in the stove as they had before, but this time, in the other stove, they put in pellets that would send white smoke, not black, over the top of the Sistine Chapel.

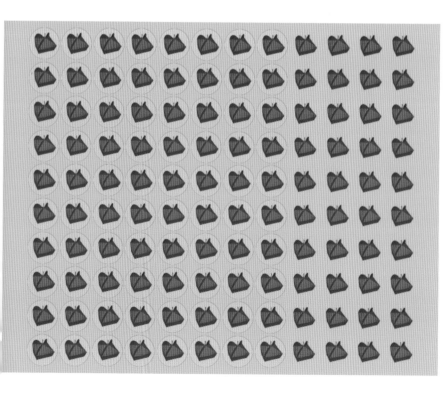

Margaret couldn't see the white smoke from where she sat.

But she heard it—and by that I mean, she heard nearly ten thousand people gathered outside in St. Peter's Square cheering at the top of their lungs with joy and excitement.

One of the cardinals had come from the conclave and stood on the central balcony of St. Peter's Basilica. He looked down upon the immense crowd of people and he said into a microphone, *"Habemus papam."*

This means, "We have a pope."

CHAPTER 5

Margaret and the Cardinals were in the Sistine Chapel, altogether, for three days. Each evening, the Cardinals would return to their rooms to sleep, elsewhere in the Vatican. They had no phones, no screens, no messages, no conversations with anyone at all other than each other. Then, the next morning, they would quietly walk back into the Sistine Chapel again.

What did Margaret eat while she remained hiding beneath those floorboards in the Chapel?

I'm glad you asked, because she was always hungry. Margaret, as you may know, likes to eat a lot.

It wasn't pizza.

She ate exactly what the Cardinals ate. Not many people know that there are nuns who live inside the Vatican and that they are the ones who prepare the food that is eaten by the College of Cardinals in conclave.

By Cardinals' standards, that food might have been simple. But, according to Margaret, it couldn't have been any better!

THE END

ABOUT THE AUTHOR

Jon M. Sweeney is an author, husband, and father of four. He has been interviewed on many television programs including CBS Saturday Morning, Fox News, and PBS's Religion and Ethics Newsweekly. His popular history *The Pope Who Quit: A True Medieval Tale of Mystery, Death, and Salvation* was optioned by HBO. He's the author of thirty-five other books, including *The Complete Francis of Assisi*, *Thomas Merton*, and *Feed the Wolf: Befriending Our Fears in the Way of Saint Francis*. The Pope's Cat series are his only books for children. He presents often at literary and religious conferences, and churches, writes regularly for *America* in the US and *The Tablet* in the UK, and is active on social media (Twitter @ jonmsweeney; Facebook jonmsweeney).

ABOUT THE ILLUSTRATOR

Roy DeLeon is an Oblate of St. Benedict, a spiritual director, a workshop facilitator focused on creative praying, an Urban Sketcher, and a professional illustrator. In addition to illustrating The Pope's Cat series, he is also the author of *Praying with the Body: Bringing the Psalms to Life*. He lives in Bothell, Washington, with his wife, Annie.

The Pope's **CAT** series

By **JON M. SWEENEY**

Illustrated by **ROY DELEON**

BOOK ONE

ISBN 978-1-61261-935-4
Trade paperback | $9.99

BOOK TWO

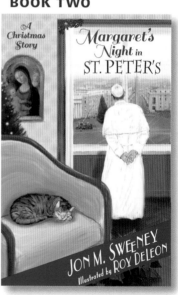

ISBN 978-1-61261-936-1
Trade paperback | $10.99

BOOK THREE

ISBN 978-1-61261-937-8
Trade paperback | $9.99

BOOK FOUR

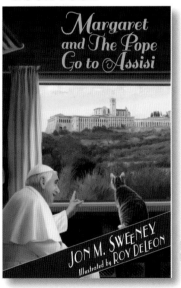

ISBN 978-1-64060-170-3
Trade paperback | $10.99